OFF THE BENCH

BY JAKE MADDOX

ILLUSTRATED BY SEAN TIFFANY

text by Eric Stevens

STONE ARCH BOOKS
a capstone imprint

Impact Books are published by Stone Arch Books
A Capstone Imprint
151 Good Counsel Drive, P.O. Box 669
Mankato, Minnesota 56002
www.capstonepub.com

Early
I
maddox
Main

Copyright © 2010 by Stone Arch Books

Printed in the United States of America in Stevens Point, Wisconsin.
092009
005619WZS10

Library of Congress Cataloging-in-Publication data is available on the Library
of Congress website.

Library Binding: 978-1-4342-1922-0
Paperback: 978-1-4342-2278-7

CREATIVE DIRECTOR: Heather Kindseth
ART DIRECTOR: Kay Fraser
GRAPHIC DESIGNER: Hilary Wacholz
PRODUCTION SPECIALIST: Michelle Biedscheid

TABLE OF CONTENTS

Team JAKE MADDOX

WILLY WILDCAT, COACH T, TREY, DANIEL, DWAYNE, ISAAC, PJ

#		Position	PPG	FT %	FG %	Stl	R
	Danny Powell	Center	9	73.2	82.8	5	2
11	Daniel Friedland	Forward	5.7	95.8	85.1	12	1
13	PJ Harris	Center	22	65.6	90.2	7	3
23	Trey Smith Ⓒ	Guard	14	96.2	80.5	20	8
26	Isaac Roth	Guard	11.5	94.1	79.3	11	6
33	Dwayne Illy	Forward	6.2	82.9	77.9	9	13

Athlete Highlight: **Daniel Friedland**

Daniel Friedland is the 5'6 second-string small forward for the Westfield Wildcats. He's skilled in foul shots and speed, but he lacks defensive knowledge. Since he's not a starter, he doesn't get enough time on the court.

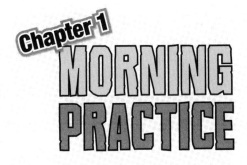

Chapter 1
MORNING PRACTICE

Daniel Friedland looked down at his sneakers. He inched up until his toes were close to the foul line, painted in white on the blacktop. He held his basketball in front of him and spun it between his palms. When he took a deep breath, the air was cold and his nose stung.

Slowly, he breathed out through his mouth. He looked at the basket through the cloud of vapor.

Then he pulled back the ball and shot.

Swish!

Daniel let himself smile. After months of coming down to the public courts every morning to practice his foul shot, he rarely missed.

Daniel pulled up the zipper of his hooded sweatshirt. It was still very cold this early in the morning. The bell to begin homeroom over at Westfield Middle School wouldn't ring for another hour.

He jogged over to the basket and grabbed the ball before it rolled onto the grass. Then he quickly walked back to the foul line.

"I think I'm as good as Dwayne Illy now," Daniel muttered to himself. "At least from the foul line."

Dwayne Illy was the starting small forward and the top scorer on the team. Most of his points, though, were from the foul line.

Daniel lifted the ball to take another shot. "If I'm ever going to start at small forward," he said to himself, "I need to be better from the line than Dwayne."

Daniel released the ball.

Swish!

He jogged to the basket and grabbed the ball as it dropped from the hoop. Quickly, he jumped up and went for a layup.

The ball hit the corner of the rim and the backboard and fell back to the blacktop.

Daniel's shoulders sagged.

"Aw, who am I kidding?" Daniel muttered. "Coach T will never start me, not with Dwayne Illy on the team."

Dejected, he put the ball under his arm and headed home to shower before school.

Chapter 2
BRICK!

Later that week, Daniel sat on the bench as the Wildcats played the Hornets from Josette Junior High. The first half had been very close, so Coach T started the five top players in the second, too.

That meant not Daniel.

Dwayne Illy drove hard to the basket and was fouled. From the line he got two points. The second half was starting just how the coach wanted.

On the next drive, Isaac Roth, starting point guard, stopped at the top of the key. He pumped once to fake a shot.

The Hornets defender was totally fooled, and Isaac got a clear pass to Dwayne as he drove the lane.

Dwayne caught the pass and laid up the ball in one motion. It was smooth.

All five starters high-fived and cheered. Daniel did his best to cheer too, but it was hard to be excited when he was spending the whole game on the bench.

The rest of the second half went just as well. Dwayne Illy got sixteen more points from the line and six from the floor.

With two minutes left in the game, the Westfield Wildcats were up by twenty points.

"All right, you guys," Coach T said to the five players on the bench, including Daniel. "Here's your chance to shine."

The five starters took a seat on the bench, and the five second-string players took the court. Daniel could tell that the other guys weren't very excited. They all knew the coach only played them when the Wildcats had the game in the bag.

"Guys," Daniel said to the other second-stringers. "Let's make the most of this."

"What do you mean?" asked Sam Yohai, the point guard.

"All we have to do is wind the clock down, right?" Daniel asked. "Well, I think we should put a few points up there. Let's show Coach T that we're as good as those starters."

Sam looked at Daniel and the other second-stringers. "But," he said slowly, "we're not."

Daniel rolled his eyes. "Listen," he said, "just get me the ball one time so I can drive. You'll see."

Play started, and Sam called a play from the top of the key. Daniel cut across the key, caught Sam's pass, and drove for the hoop.

Daniel's defender gave him enough space, and Daniel went for the layup.

Brick!

With a thud, the ball slapped into the bottom of the rim and fell hard, right into the hands of the Hornets center. He heaved the ball up the court to the Hornets star player, who scored easily.

"All right, guys," Coach T called. He looked right at Daniel. "That's enough showing off out there. Just hold the lead, okay?"

Daniel sighed. *Great*, he thought. *This was my chance, and I messed it up.*

"See?" Sam said. "Let's just finish this."

Daniel shook his head. "I guess this is why we're second-string," he mumbled.

Chapter 3
STARTING?

"From one bench to another bench," Daniel muttered. He was sitting on the plank of wood, held up by two iron posts, in front of his locker after the game. He sighed.

"Talking to yourself again, Friedland?" Dwayne Illy said. Daniel hadn't noticed him walking by.

"What?" Daniel said. "Oh, no, I'm just, um, thinking."

"None of my business," Dwayne said, stopping him. Then he walked on, into Coach Turnbull's office.

"I really have to stop talking to myself," Daniel said quietly. Then he reached into his locker for his street clothes.

No need to shower, he thought. *One drive to the hoop isn't enough for me to break a sweat.*

As he pulled off his team jersey, he overheard Dwayne and the coach talking.

"All week?" the coach said. "That means you'll miss our game against Killcreek!"

"I know, Coach T," Dwayne replied. "But I can't do anything about it. The whole family is going to visit my aunt in Arlington. It's the annual Illy family reunion."

The coach sighed loudly. "I don't like this at all, Dwayne. Can't your whole family wait until school vacation, like everyone else?" Coach T said.

"Last year, my cousins missed school, but our school was on break," Dwayne explained. "This year, it's my turn. Our school schedules are different."

The coach's chair creaked. "Well, it can't be helped, I guess," Coach Turnbull said. "I guess we can survive one week without the great Dwayne Illy."

Dwayne laughed. "I don't know about that," he said.

Daniel heard the coach's door close. He pulled on his shirt and acted like he hadn't been listening. When Dwayne walked by, Daniel didn't even look at him.

Once Dwayne was out of earshot, Daniel dropped back onto the bench. "Well," he muttered, "maybe I'll get to start at small forward after all."

He grabbed his jeans from his locker. "Of course, with the way I drove today," he added, "I'm not so sure I want to."

Chapter 4
NERVES

Daniel decided to walk home from school that day. He usually rode the late bus, but it was a nice afternoon, and the bus was always loud. The walk would give him some time to think.

The walk home wasn't very long. Daniel practiced his dribbling skills as he walked, sometimes just bouncing his ball at his side, sometimes switching hands suddenly, through his legs.

When Daniel reached his house, he stopped in the driveway and continued to practice his dribbling. A few minutes later, he heard a car horn and looked up. His dad was waiting to drive into the driveway.

"Hi, Dad," Daniel called out. He moved to the side to let his father park.

The old car's brakes squeaked as it stopped. The door creaked as Dad climbed out. "I hope you finished your homework," Dad said. "Otherwise I know you wouldn't be out here playing ball."

"Actually, I just got home," Daniel replied. He stopped dribbling and held the ball under his arm. "I decided to walk home today."

Together, Daniel and his father headed up the sidewalk and into the house.

Inside, Dad grabbed the mail off the floor just inside the door. As he flipped through it, he said, "Something on your mind?"

Daniel dropped his sweatshirt and basketball in the front closet. "Yes," he said. "You know Dwayne Illy?"

"Do I know Dwayne?" Dad repeated. "Of course I do. He's the one who's been keeping my son on the bench. What about him?"

"Well, he'll be on vacation for our next game," Daniel replied. "So I think I'll be starting at small forward against Killcreek."

Dad smiled. "That's great, Danny," he said. "This is your chance to show that coach what you're made of, what you can do out there!"

"Um, it sure is," Daniel said. He hadn't meant to keep anything from his father, but he couldn't tell him how bad he was at driving the lane. Or about how he'd missed his one chance to score during the game.

"So, that's all I wanted to tell you," Daniel said, going for the stairs. "I better get up there and get my homework done before dinner, huh?"

He zoomed up to his room before his father could reply.

Chapter 5
NOT READY

At practice the next afternoon, Daniel was feeling nervous. He knew Coach Turnbull might talk to him about starting at the next game. He also knew he had embarrassed himself in the last game when he tried to drive to the basket.

The team was in their practice uniforms, sitting on the bleachers. Coach T was standing on the court looking at his clipboard.

"All right, guys," Coach T said. "Some bad news: Dwayne Illy will not be in school for a week starting this Thursday. That means he won't be around to play in the game against Killcreek on Thursday afternoon."

The team groaned. Daniel gulped.

"Aw, man, Dwayne!" Isaac Roth said. "You can't miss the game."

Dwayne shrugged. "It's not my choice, guys," he said. "What can I do?"

"Everyone settle down," Coach Turnbull said. "We have a second-string team because sometimes guys can't make the game. Daniel Friedland will start at small forward."

A few guys groaned again. Daniel slouched on the bleachers.

"Daniel's foul shot has really improved this season," Coach Turnbull went on, ignoring the groans. "He's going to be a real asset from the line."

Daniel was glad to hear the coach say that, but he could still feel the eyes of his teammates on him. No one was happy Dwayne wouldn't be around for the Killcreek game.

And to be honest, Daniel thought, *I'm not so happy about it either.*

After about a half hour of practice, Coach Turnbull gave a couple of sharp blows on his whistle. "Dwayne," he called out. "Take ten minutes. Do some laps or something."

"Seriously, Coach T?" Dwayne said. He spun the basketball on one finger. "I'm in the middle of drills."

"I see that," the coach replied. "And I want Daniel to take over at small forward in the drills for a little while."

Daniel looked up from the other end of the gym. He and the second-string players had been playing some half court.

"You got it, Coach," Dwayne said. He tossed the ball to Isaac and started a lap.

Daniel looked over at the other second-stringers. Sam shrugged at him.

"Looks like you've been promoted," Sam said. "For now."

Daniel sighed and walked down the court toward Isaac and the other starters.

"Hi," Daniel said.

The four boys looked at him, then at each other. "Let's do this," Isaac said.

Isaac dribbled up to the top of the key and raised his right hand, showing two fingers.

Daniel knew what he was supposed to do. It was the same play Daniel had seen Isaac and Dwayne do in lots of games during the season.

Isaac would fake a shot, Dwayne would cut across the key, and Isaac would move up the left side as he passed the ball to Dwayne. Then Dwayne was supposed to drive hard to the hoop.

"I can do this," Daniel muttered to himself.

Daniel looked at Isaac. Isaac pumped once, then cut to his left. Daniel quickly ran across the key just as Isaac's pass came through.

Daniel caught the pass, spun, and drove to the hoop.

On his last dribble before the shot, though, the ball hit his forward foot and flew out of bounds.

Coach Turnbull blew his whistle.

"You feeling all right, Daniel?" the coach called out.

"I'm fine," Daniel replied. He looked at Isaac. "Let's take it from the top. Sorry."

Isaac shook his head as the assistant coach tossed the ball back in. Then he held up two fingers again to start the play.

Daniel cut across the key and caught the pass just fine. He looked down the lane, and drove to the hoop. He went up for the layup . . .

Brick!

The ball thudded hard into the side of the hoop and ricocheted into the bleachers. Coach Turnbull's whistle was piercing this time.

"Daniel," he called out. "Come over here."

Daniel took a deep breath and jogged over to the coach.

"I know, I know," Daniel said as he stepped up to the coach. "I must just be a little nervous."

Coach Turnbull put a hand on Daniel's shoulder. "Scott Dean has been working hard on his ball handling," the coach said. Scott was a second-string guard.

"Um," Daniel said, "yeah, he's gotten pretty good."

"Scott might have a little less trouble with those drives that are breaking up your game this afternoon," Coach T went on.

"Wait a minute," Daniel said. "What are you saying?"

The coach sighed. "Your foul shot has really improved. Everyone's noticed," he said. "But maybe you're not quite ready to start at small forward after all."

Chapter 6
GIVE UP

"I don't know what to do," Daniel said. He was walking home again, but this time his friend Jimmy Kim was walking with him. Jimmy was the sports writer for the school newspaper.

"This might be my only chance to start, since Dwayne is out of town," Daniel said. "But let's face it. I'm not good enough. Maybe it would be easier to just let Scott take my place."

Jimmy shrugged. "I suppose it would be easier," he said.

"You think I should just give up?" Daniel asked, a little surprised.

"I didn't say that," Jimmy said. "I just agreed it would be easier to give up."

"Oh, I see," Daniel said with a roll of his eyes. "You're being wise, huh?"

Jimmy laughed. "It's the only way I know how to be," he said. "Look, my point is this. From the line you're as good as Dwayne Illy, right?"

Daniel shrugged. "Might be," he said.

Jimmy waved him off. "I've seen his stats," he said, "and yours. Plus I've seen you at the park, just shooting foul shot after foul shot. You're as good, probably better."

"Okay," Daniel said.

"Now, your game from the floor," Jimmy went on, "that's another story."

"You're telling me," Daniel said. "I'm a mess."

"You're not that bad," Jimmy said. "I get that practice didn't go so well, but I know you don't normally dribble off your own foot. You're better than that. It sounds like today was way worse than normal."

"Man, it was awful," Daniel said, remembering how embarrassed he'd been at practice.

"You do throw a heck of a brick now and then, though," Jimmy added.

"Hey!" Daniel protested. But it was true, he knew it.

"So, you've got four days," Jimmy went on. "It's not ideal, but you can practice, and get your drive down."

"You want me to just stroll up to Coach T and say, 'Hey, Coach. I have to practice my game from the floor, so let's just focus on me between now and game day'?" Daniel said.

The two boys reached the corner of Main and Eighth Street. Jimmy's family lived to the left, and Daniel's to the right.

"Look, I gotta head home," Jimmy said. "But you worked on your foul shot all season without help from the coach or the practices. Why can't you do the same with your drives? Anyway, I'll see you."

Daniel stood on the corner as Jimmy walked away.

"He's right," Daniel muttered to himself. "I've done it before. I can do it again."

He turned to his right and started toward home. To his surprise, a group of old men were sitting on a nearby bench, watching him.

"Also," he added quickly, "I really have to stop talking to myself."

Chapter 7
HELP!

The next morning, Daniel was up early, as always. He headed to the park to practice. But that morning, instead of shooting foul shot after foul shot, Daniel practiced his layups.

He stood at the top of the key, then dribbled up one side of the lane. He tried not to think about bouncing the ball off his foot, or throwing up a brick. He tried to just focus on making the shots.

As he reached the bottom of the key, he jumped, raised the ball, and gently released it. It hit the backboard, circled the rim, and fell out.

"Well," Daniel said, grabbing the rebound, "better than last time, at least."

For an hour, Daniel took layup after layup, sometimes from the left and sometimes from the right. By the end of his practice session, he had made a few shots.

Still, it wasn't quite what he needed. He needed to make all the shots.

* * *

When Daniel got to school later that morning, he found PJ Harris and Isaac Roth hanging out by their lockers.

"Hi, PJ. Hey, Isaac," he said.

The two starters looked at him for a moment.

"What's up, Daniel?" Isaac said.

"You guys know I, um, might be starting in the next game, right?" Daniel asked.

Isaac and PJ looked at each other, then nodded.

"Listen, I know I'm not the best ball handler on the team," Daniel went on.

Isaac laughed. "Not even close," he said. PJ chuckled.

Daniel pretended he hadn't heard that. "But my foul shot is good," he said. "Jimmy Kim thinks I might have the best shot from the line on the team."

Isaac seemed impressed. But he said, "So what's your point?"

"I need your help, both of you," Daniel said. "PJ, you can block anything, practically, since you're the tallest guy on the team."

"Tallest in the league," PJ corrected him.

"Okay," Daniel said, turning to Isaac. "And you're the best defender on the team, right?"

"Most steals in the league since the 1980s," Isaac said, smiling.

"Right," Daniel said. "But PJ, you also get called for shooting fouls, and Isaac, you get called for reaching in."

"You better have a point," PJ said, frowning down at Daniel.

"I want to practice driving on you two," Daniel said quickly, "so I can play well in the game, and get to the foul line to score."

Isaac and PJ looked at Daniel for a long time. A bell rang, letting them know homeroom would be starting in two minutes.

"So?" Daniel asked nervously. "Will you help?"

"The game is in three days," Isaac replied. "How are we going to have time to practice, just the three of us?"

"I'm at the park courts every day at six," Daniel replied.

"Man, I can't go practice at six," PJ said. "I have dinner with my dad, and then do my homework."

"No, six in the morning," Daniel explained.

Isaac and PJ just about fell over. "In the morning?" Isaac said. "That's insane!"

"It's how I got my foul shot so good," Daniel said. "Look, we better get to homeroom. Think about it. And then be at the court at six tomorrow morning."

With that, Daniel jogged down the hall and got to class just in time.

Chapter 8
TWO-ON-ONE

The next morning, the grass was wet, and a mist hung over the court. Daniel jogged up with his hood on and his coat zipped up to his neck.

He was almost surprised to see two people on the court already. One of them was very, very tall.

"Hey," Isaac called to him. "We were afraid you weren't showing up."

"It would have been the meanest prank ever," PJ added. "There would have been revenge."

Daniel laughed. "Well, I made it, so please don't hurt me," he said. He went right to the foul line, raised his ball, and sank an easy swish.

"Nice shot," PJ said.

Isaac grabbed the rebound and passed it to Daniel. "Courtesy," he said.

Daniel dribbled once, then shot. Another swish.

This time PJ grabbed the rebound. "You ever miss?" he asked. He passed the ball back to Daniel.

Daniel spun the ball between his palms. "Sure," he said. "Watch this."

He drove up the left side of the lane and tried for the layup. The ball hit the center of the backboard and fell past the other side of the rim.

"See?" Daniel said. He jogged after the ball as it rolled off the court.

"And that's why we're here," Isaac said. "Right?"

"Exactly," Daniel replied. "If I can score from the floor, there's a chance the defense will foul me. And we know I can score from the line."

"Then what are we waiting for?" Isaac said. "Let's play a little two-on-one."

Chapter 9
TWO FROM THE FLOOR

Daniel met with PJ and Isaac on the courts for the next two mornings. By the time team practice came around the day before the game, Daniel was feeling pretty good about his layups.

The team sat on the bleachers and Coach Turnbull stood before them. "To get ready for game day, and to help me choose a starting small forward," he said, "we're going to play some five-on-five today."

Coach T looked at his clipboard. "Now, as you probably noticed, Dwayne Illy is off to his family reunion already," the coach went on, "so at small forward on the red team will be Daniel Friedland. For the blue team, Scott Dean will play small forward."

Daniel looked at Scott. He was obviously surprised to hear his name called, since he was normally a guard.

"The four starters, split between red and blue," Coach T said, "and the rest of the second-string, fill in the gaps. Let's get started."

PJ and Isaac both ended up on Daniel's team. They both gave him a high five after they'd all pulled on their red scrimmage jerseys.

"You feel ready?" Isaac asked.

Daniel nodded. "Definitely," he said. "Those guys don't know what they're in for."

Daniel was right.

The coach blew his whistle to start play. The red team got possession first and PJ passed to Isaac.

Isaac held the ball at the top of the key, looking for Daniel. Isaac held up two fingers, calling the play.

Daniel cut across the key and caught Isaac's pass. He spun to his left, then to his right. Then he drove to the hoop.

Hank Jones, the second-string center, barely tried to stop the drive. Like the rest of the team, he thought Daniel was no good from the floor. But Daniel surprised everyone.

With one long step, Daniel jumped. He loosely let the ball glide off his hand. It hit the backboard gently and fell in for two points.

"Nice one, Daniel," PJ called.

Isaac held up his palm for a high five. "Nice layup," he said.

Daniel slapped his hand. "Now they know I can shoot," he said.

Isaac nodded. "So now we go with plan B," he said.

Chapter 10
NEW STARTER

On the blue team's first possession, Scott proved what a great ball handler he was. He took a pass outside the key, then drove to the hoop. He fooled three defenders and went for a layup. PJ was right in his face, though.

Coach T blew his whistle. "Foul," he called. "Watch the arm, PJ."

So Scott went to the line.

Daniel already knew Scott's ball handling was great, but he hadn't seen him shoot too many foul shots before. Scott stood at the line, took a deep breath, and shot. The ball hit the backboard too low. It launched off the back of the rim, right back to Scott.

"One more, one more," the coach said. "Make it a good one."

The players on the sides of the lane got ready to go for the rebound. PJ bounced lightly on his toes. Scott raised the ball for his second shot and let it go.

PJ jumped and got the rebound. Daniel turned and headed up the court. PJ's pass was perfect. Daniel took it right to the hoop, but Hank Jones was right next to him. The coach's whistle sounded again.

"Foul, Hank," Coach T said. "Take the line, Daniel."

"This is our game now," Isaac said, smiling. Scott gave him a nasty look.

Coach T handed Daniel the ball. Daniel spun it between his palms and faced the basket. He raised the ball, exhaled, and shot.

Swish!

"Nice shot," Isaac said, clapping. "Nice shot."

"One more," the coach said. PJ tossed the rebound to the coach, who handed the ball to Daniel.

Daniel held the ball up, lined up the shot, and let it go. The ball hit the backboard softly and fell in.

"That's two more points," Coach Turnbull said. "Blue ball."

* * *

Daniel went on to score twenty points in the scrimmage. The red team beat the blue team easily. At the end of practice, Daniel, Isaac, and PJ were celebrating. Coach Turnbull went over to them.

"Daniel, come talk to me for a minute," Coach Turnbull said. Isaac and PJ slapped Daniel on the back as he followed the coach over to the bench.

"What's up, Coach T?" Daniel said. He took a seat on the bench and faced his coach.

"So, Daniel," Coach Turnbull said, "you sure have improved a lot, especially on those layups."

"Thanks," Daniel said. "But I don't deserve all the credit. Isaac and PJ practiced with me a lot the last few days."

The coach looked surprised. "They did?" he asked. "When?"

"They met me at the public courts before school," Daniel said. "I'm always down there, usually to practice free throws."

"I'm really impressed with your attitude, Daniel," the coach said. "That makes me even more sure of this decision. I have no problem with starting you in the game tomorrow. I'm sure you'll do well."

"Thanks, Coach T," Daniel replied.

"Dwayne is going to move up to the high school team next year," the coach said. "That means I'll be looking for a new starting forward!"

Daniel's mouth dropped open. "Really?" he asked.

The coach nodded. "That's right," he said. "So how would you like to be our new small forward?"

Daniel jumped to his feet and smiled. "That would be great!" he said. "I'll keep practicing too, every morning."

The coach laughed. "I believe it," he said. "Now go get showered and rest up for tomorrow. Maybe take tomorrow morning off, huh?"

Daniel headed to the locker room and opened his locker. His uniform was there, still nearly as clean as the day he got it.

"I'll have to bring that home after tomorrow's game," he said to himself. "I'll finally break a sweat on game day."

THE AUTHOR
ERIC STEVENS

15

ERIC STEVENS LIVES IN ST. PAUL, MINNESOTA WITH HIS WIFE, DOG, AND SON. HE IS STUDYING TO BECOME A TEACHER. SOME OF HIS FAVORITE THINGS INCLUDE PIZZA AND VIDEO GAMES. SOME OF HIS LEAST FAVORITE THINGS INCLUDE OLIVES AND SHOVELING SNOW.

24

THE ILLUSTRATOR
SEAN TIFFANY

WHEN SEAN TIFFANY WAS GROWING UP, HE LIVED ON A SMALL ISLAND OFF THE COAST OF MAINE. EVERY DAY UNTIL HE GRADUATED FROM HIGH SCHOOL, HE HAD TO TAKE A BOAT TO GET TO SCHOOL! SEAN HAS A PET CACTUS NAMED JIM.

GLOSSARY

asset (ASS-et)—something or someone that is helpful or useful

defense (DI-fenss)—the team guarding the basket

earshot (EER-shot)—within hearing distance

focus (FOH-kuhss)—to concentrate on something

possession (puh-ZESH-uhn)—when one team has control of the ball

reunion (ree-YOON-yuhn)—a gathering

ricocheted (RIK-uh-shayd)—hit a hard surface and bounced off in another direction

schedules (SKEJ-ulz)—arrangements of time

scrimmage (SKRIM-ij)—a game played for practice

second-stringer (SEK-uhnd STRING-ur)—someone who is not a starter

DISCUSSION QUESTIONS

1. Daniel isn't afraid to ask for help. What else could he have done to improve his skills?

2. Daniel jokes that he talks to himself too much. What do you think?

3. Who is the most important player on the Wildcats team? Why?

WRITING PROMPTS

1. This book ends before the big game. What do you think happens in the game? Write about it.

2. Write about a time when you needed help to learn a new skill. Who helped you? What happened?

3. Are you on a team? Write about the members of your team.

MORE ABOUT SMALL FORWARDS

In this book, Daniel Friedland is a small forward for the Westfield Wildcats. Check out these quick facts about small forwards.

* Small forwards need to be fast and able to score. They also have to be able to defend well. Because they must have many different skills on the court, small forwards are considered the most flexible players in basketball.

* Small forwards aren't usually the tallest players on the team, but some small forwards are just as tall as centers. In the NBA, the average small forward is between 6'5 and 6'10.

* Famous small forwards include Scottie Pippen, Shawn Marion, Tayshaun Prince, Trevor Ariza, LeBron James, Larry Bird, and Julius Erving.